Ravi and the
Tales of Tunnel Town

Peter Erlam

Cover Design by Jo Knowles

Published by New Generation Publishing in 2022

First Edition

Paperback ISBN: 978-1-80369-368-2

www.newgeneration-publishing.com

 New Generation Publishing

For the children of Ukraine and all the world's young,
voiceless victims of conflict and persecution

Preface

Prime Minister Winston Churchill emerges from a bomb-damaged Ramsgate hotel, cigar in hand, seconds before the air raid sirens warn of an imminent attack.

In peacetime, an August weekend in the seaside resort of Ramsgate would normally conjure up images of happy holidaymakers on packed beaches.

But this was 1940, the country was at war, and the 24th of August would be remembered not as a bucket 'n' spade day but as 'Black Saturday' - the day that German planes dropped 500 bombs on the town, causing death and destruction on a massive scale.

Five days later, Prime Minister Winston Churchill, on a tour of the South coast, was driven from Dover to Ramsgate to inspect the devastation caused by the Luftwaffe.

That afternoon, when Mr Churchill stepped out of a damaged hotel near the town's harbour, an air raid siren sounded, warning of an imminent aerial attack.

Immediately, the Mayor escorted his VIP guest to the Queen Street entrance to the Tunnels, a network of shelters, a few minutes' walk away.

But, on his way, Mr Churchill had lit one of his trademark cigars. Near to the access, he was reminded there was strictly no smoking underground.

The PM was not happy - he loved his Cuban cigars and was rarely seen in public without one - but on this occasion he had no choice. "There goes a good 'un," he sighed as he stubbed it out under his heel.

A small crowd had gathered to catch a glimpse of their wartime leader and several of them scrambled to retrieve the discarded cigar. There could not have been a more treasured souvenir of his visit, and it soon disappeared in the frantic scrummage.

Though details of Mr Churchill's visit to Ramsgate were widely reported in the newspapers, nothing more was heard about what happened to his 'good 'un' - the cigar he had to throw away.

PREMIER'S VISIT.

MR. WINSTON CHURCHILL THROWS AWAY A CIGAR.

The Premier, Mr. Winston Churchill, paid a visit to Ramsgate on Wednesday afternoon, and received a most enthusiastic welcome from those who were fortunate enough to catch a glimpse of him.

Accompanied by the Mayor (Alderman A. B. C. Kempe), Mr. Churchill made a tour of inspection of the areas damaged during the recent air raids and evinced the utmost interest in everything he saw.

Afterwards, the Mayor told us that Mr. Churchill was particularly concerned with the position of those who had been rendered homeless by the raid, and expressed the opinion that the Governmnt should do everything possible to see that no one suffered unduly.

He visited a restaurant which had been badly damaged by an air raid which took place only a few hours before his arrival.

Hearing that the proprietor had been injured and was in hospital, Mr. Churchill, who had been introduced to Miss Nellie Wiles, the head waitress, asked after the injured man and expressed his pleasure that he was progressing favourably.

As he was leaving the premises an air raid warning sounded and Mr. Churchill took refuge in the town's tunnel shelters.

Characteristically, he was smoking a cigar during his visit, but as he approached the tunnel entrance he was informed by the Mayor that smoking was not allowed in the shelters.

Promptly he took the cigar from his mouth. "There goes a good 'un," he said ruefully, as he dropped it on the sanded floor.

After leaving Ramsgate, which he did

An article in the East Kent Times tells how Mr Churchill was told to stub out his cigar before entering the tunnel shelter.

Chapter 1

An explosion of joy

RAMSGATE, Summer 2021

It's coming home

   It's coming home

   Football's coming home…

Wave after wave of full-throated chanting drifted across Ellington Park, drowning out all other sounds in the salty sea air. England had just scored again and were edging closer to victory.

Bump! A champagne cork bounced off the branch where Ravi was perched. The raven had planned for an early sleep on this starry night, but there was no chance of that now.

"Wow, the humans are really excited about something tonight," he observed, rearranging his shiny black feathers.

The streets of Ramsgate were filled with happy humans. Most of them were wearing white and red shirts and waving flags of the same colours.

The triumphant 'coming home' song had been heard on other evenings during the previous two weeks. But tonight was different - and much noisier.

England were playing Germany at Wembley. England had scored twice in the second half to earn a place in the next round of the Euro Championships. Ravi had not experienced such scenes of excitement since moving from London to east Kent.

Coincidentally, Ravi had his own reasons to celebrate. That week, he had been hailed a hero on the front page of the local newspaper, the Thanet Gazette.

Round his neck was a medal awarded to him for his part in helping to rescue a local lad, Tom, after he had fallen from a coastal path down a cliff.

Tom and his pal Wills, both aged 9, were friends with Evie, also 9, and her younger sister Tilda, aged 8. They all lived within a short walk of each other in the town's Ellington Road.

The girls and their parents, Mike and Tamara Green, were caught up in the football fever that had gripped the nation. And tonight, when the referee blew for full-time, their entire neighbourhood let rip.

It was an explosion of joy after more than a year of uncertainty and confinement caused by Covid-19. Fireworks were fizzing and crackling, creating a panoply of colour in the night sky.

Another champagne cork popped. It came from the house next door to the Greens, where Ravi had made his home at the top of an old conifer tree a few months earlier, when he had flown off to escape from the capital – and its pigeons.

"I moved here for a bit of peace and quiet. I'm

not going to get any of that tonight!" Ravi reflected as he watched the second cork spin through the branches.

The following morning, motorists were sounding their horns. Even more cars than usual were adorned with St George's stickers and pennants.

And despite many England supporters having lost sleep, there was still an extra spring in the step of those who had stayed up late to watch their team's historic victory.

In a few weeks, the Green sisters and their friends would start their summer break but that morning Evie and Wills had their regular Wednesday history lesson with their favourite teacher, Mr Smith.

Last term, they had learned about the Anglo-Saxon origin of Ramsgate's name, meaning 'ravens cliff gap'. This part of Kent had been an established raven habitat for many hundreds of years but last century the population had declined steeply. It was only in the past dozen or so years that ravens had reappeared.

As the class settled for the start of the lesson, Mr Smith wanted to update his pupils on recent events involving one of their classmates. "You'll have noticed that Tom is not here today. He's still at home recovering from his injuries in last week's fall. He's ok and hopes to be back with us next week."

Evie put her hand up. She had more news for the class. "When Tilda and I called to see him this morning before school he told us that Ravi had been visiting him in the garden. They've become really good pals.

"Tom feeds him scraps of meat as a thank-you and says to him: 'Thank you. You saved my life'. Ravi has now started to repeat that, and other phrases Tom uses regularly."

"Yes, that's typical of ravens," said Mr Smith. "They're like parrots in that sense. But you've got to be careful what you say in front of them as they might repeat something you wouldn't want your parents to hear."

At this point, Mr Smith announced it was time to focus on the day's topic. "In the light of last night's football match, I want us to look at Ramsgate's historic links with Germany, both good and bad."

"Yeah, what a great win, sir!" said Wills, without realising he had interrupted his teacher.

"My grandad was so excited. He had been at the old Wembley stadium to see the World Cup final in 1966 when England beat Germany 4-1. He was the same age as me then - and we haven't won the World Cup since!"

"Thanks for that, Wills," smiled Mr Smith. "Even though your story is a painful reminder of England's long wait for football glory!"

Undaunted, their teacher continued: "Today, I want us to focus on one of the darkest days in our town's past, the day that Ramsgate was heavily bombed by the Luftwaffe, which was the

German equivalent of our Royal Air Force.

"Nowadays, of course, we are great friends with the German nation; German children have been coming here to learn English at Thanet's language schools for a long time and, during their stay, are hosted by local families.

"There are several German students who have kept in touch with their hosts after their initial visit. Several have become lifelong friends.

"But it has not always been that way. When Germany invaded Poland in September 1939 it led to the start of World War II, which dragged on for six years until the Allied countries defeated the Nazis in 1945."

Evie's hand shot up. "But, Mr Smith, why did the Germans want to drop bombs on Ramsgate. It was just a small fishing town, a long way from London?"

"Good question, Evie. But before I answer it, I first want to tell you about a very interesting character called Mr A.B.C. Kempe, who at the time was known as Ramsgate's 'Mad Mayor.'"

As usual, Mr Smith had managed to grab the class's attention.

"Of course you're thinking, why 'mad' mayor? Well, he used to do unexpected things such as wear a top hat on the beach...

Suddenly, there was a tapping on the classroom window near to where Evie was sitting. It was Ravi. In his beak was a tube, about the size of a Smarties tube. But it sounded metallic, not cardboard.

None of the children were paying attention to Mr Smith any longer, certainly not Evie. She knew straight away that Ravi was trying to get a message to her. She had no idea what the message might be, but it wouldn't be the first time Ravi had raised an alert in this way.

Five minutes later, when the bell rang to signal the end of the lesson, Evie headed out to find her younger sister Tilda to let her know the latest Ravi news.

Chapter 2

Ravi is still a rascal

LONDON Summer 2021

"Did you see the picture of that rascal raven in the Metro yesterday?" One London pigeon was chatting to another about Ravi's heroics on the Kent coast, 70 miles away.

Chatter about events in Ramsgate had already spread among the capital's bird population, even before the newspapers were aware of the story.

Ravi had emerged as the key figure in the search for young Tom. After locating the stranded boy, he carried a message from Tom back to the Greens' house. The family alerted the police and the air ambulance's recovery operation ensured the tale had a happy ending.

Now, the two pigeons, James and Toby, both with their chests puffed up, were discussing the raven's role in the dramatic cliffside rescue and his award of a Distinguished Flying Cross.

The irony of it all was not lost on the pair of pigeons. They remembered him as a bird with a tarnished reputation. Ravi had been a member of the elite team of ravens at the Tower of London but was dismissed for bad conduct.

Basically, he was thrown out for being a nuisance to visitors - nothing serious, just being mischievous.

"Now, he's strutting around like one of us," announced James. "Did you notice, in that photo, that he was holding his head at a cocky angle."

Toby replied, in a mocking tone: "Yes, you're right. Ravi looked well pleased with himself. He even had a medal round his neck.

"But what about his bad behaviour? He had a funny habit of pinching people's possessions and attacking TV aerials. No wonder young Ravi was packed off to a zoo."

James added: "Last thing I heard he escaped from the zoo, got fed up with life in London and flew off to make a fresh start by the sea. Good luck to him.

"Mind you, Ravi never had a high opinion of us pigeons. But, heh, the feeling was mutual."

Rikki, one of Ravi's best raven friends in London, was eavesdropping on the pigeons' conversation, high up in an oak tree beside the river Thames.

"Yes, that's right, James," said Rikki. "But It's not pigeons themselves that Ravi doesn't like, it's the way you always seem to be spoilt by the tourists. They always feed you and 'coo-coo' at you. It's as if you are the only birds in London.

"So, I suppose Ravi did have a thing about pigeons. He was always moaning about you. But now he's at the seaside he'll no doubt be complaining about the noisy seagulls instead.

That's just the way he is," said Rikki.

Looking along the branch to the pigeons, Rikki added: "I'll be able to give you an update soon. I'm planning to visit Ravi in his new home. I'll pass on your best wishes," the raven chuckled.

"Don't bother!" said Toby, tossing his head back.

* * * *

Meanwhile, in Ramsgate, Ravi was puzzled about why Evie had not come out of the school building to see him.

Since making friends with the Green sisters earlier in summer he had usually been able to get their attention by tapping on their bedroom window, usually with a coin in his beak.

So he wondered why Evie had ignored him when he tapped on the classroom window.

Ravi was a brainy raven - the cleverest of the

Corvid bird species - but, of course, he had never attended a human school. So, he did not understand that students were not allowed to walk out of a lesson without a very good reason.

When Ravi had struck the classroom window several times with the tube, Mr Smith, who had by now lost the students' attention, walked over to the window, pushed it open and clapped his hands loudly.

The sudden noise startled Ravi, who dropped the tube into the flower bed below the window and flew off towards the town centre.

That afternoon, after the classroom kerfuffle, Evie could not wait to tell Tilda about Ravi's latest antics.

"It was so funny, sis. But Mr Smith was not amused. He was talking about a serious subject, to do with Ramsgate during the war, when Ravi appeared on the windowsill tapping the glass with something metallic.

"Nobody was paying Mr Smith any attention;

Ravi was causing a serious distraction. In the end, Mr Smith lost his temper and stomped over to the window, flung it open and scared off poor Ravi by clapping."

"Wow, he is a rascal, isn't he!" said Tilda. "I've noticed he's followed us to school a couple of times this week. His routine seems to be that he flies down our road to Tom's house while we are at home having breakfast. Then, when we set off for school, Ravi obviously hears us talking and he follows us."

Evie laughed: "Maybe he won't be so keen to follow us after the reception he got from Mr Smith today."

Tilda added: "I wonder what that tapping on the window was all about? It might have been something important. Last time he did something like that it resulted in us finding Tom after his fall down the cliff from the Pegwell path."

That day, Ravi had been the bearer of good

news when he flew back to the Greens' house with Tom's note. It had explained where he was on the cliff, stranded and in pain.

"That was enough excitement to last us for a while," smiled Evie. "We don't want any more drama on that scale," she added.

Chapter 3

'Mad Mayor' saves the town

RAMSGATE Summer 1940

But Tom's misadventure was nothing compared to the devastating drama of the war years. To fully understand this, the Green sisters would have to turn the clock back more than 80 years to a time when Kent was known as 'Bomb Alley'.

In peacetime, the county was referred to as the Garden of England. But the outbreak of war had changed its image, as it was directly under the shortest route for aircraft flying between Germany and London, and back.

The enemy planes' return flights were where the problems lay. There are many stories of raids over the town when Luftwaffe pilots returning from un-completed missions were ordered to offload their unused bombs over Ramsgate rather than carry them back to Germany.

In the space of five minutes on August 24, an estimated 500 bombs were dropped on the town. The newspapers labelled it the 'Murder Raid' and the day was known as 'Black Saturday'.

Hundreds of houses were either flattened or left unfit for habitation. Thirty-one people - two soldiers and 29 civilians - were killed.

But the number of dead and injured could have been far worse, had it not been for one man, Mr A.B.C. Kempe, nicknamed the 'Mad Mayor'. But he wasn't mad in a crazy way - he was just an extrovert who knew how to get things done.

Crucially, he was the driving force behind the creation of air raid shelters that saved the lives of so many Ramsgate residents.

For, as well as being a flamboyant character, the mayor with the memorable initials also had foresight and persistence.

Several years before the outbreak of World War II in 1939, Ramsgate people had expressed concern over the need for effective protection from aerial attack. They had painful memories of this new form of warfare from 20 years earlier when Zeppelin airships were used to drop bombs on the town during the First World War.

In those days, citizens soon realised the best place to be during such an attack was underground, in one of the town's many chalk caves and dugouts, originally created for farm storage and as hiding places for smugglers' goods.

The safety they provided was not forgotten by townsfolk and, in the 1930s, as Adolf Hitler's Nazi party were rising to power, Ramsgate's Borough Engineer, Dick Brimmell, drew up plans for a system of tunnels that would take full advantage of the chalk bedrock on which the town was built.

Mr Brimmell's final design included over two

miles of tunnels with entrances at strategic points around the town, which would mean everyone was within five minutes' walk of accessing subterranean safety.

But it needed Mr Kempe to persuade central government to make the funds available.

He was already an Alderman - a high-ranking member of Ramsgate Council - before being elected Mayor in 1938.

By then, the government had twice rejected the council's tunnel plan as being unnecessary and premature. This puzzled the good folk of Ramsgate, especially as Germany had already occupied Austria that year.

When Hitler's intentions regarding Europe became clear, the plan was submitted a third time to the Home Office. Mr Kempe took on the task of getting the scheme approved. He and Mr Brimmell attended a meeting in London, arranged by the area's MP, and put forward a forceful case. It was finally approved in 1939.

Construction started in March and was finished the same year. Just in time, as it turned out. The 'Murder Raid' bombardment the following summer destroyed or badly damaged 1,200 properties, causing widespread homelessness.

The tunnels were only intended to be used as shelter during air raids but by the end of 1940, these 'temporary' homes had become known as 'Tunnel Town'. More than 900 people - around 300 families - lived there, with some staying for the duration of the war.

Eventually, Tunnel Town had its own shops, barbers, canteens, and a makeshift hospital. Even dances were held there as the displaced population made a big effort to continue life as normal below ground.

Chapter 4

Ravi wins staring match

RAMSGATE Summer 2021

"Look Tom," said Wills, pointing to two small, open-topped barrels, "they even had toilets down here!"

The boys were on a tour of Ramsgate Tunnels, which since 2014 has been a major tourist attraction, open all year round. What was once a derelict railway line and then a 1940s' bomb shelter had been transformed through the hard work and dedication of volunteers.

As it was nearly the end of term, Tom - now recovered from his fall - had been given the morning off school for the trip, which was a pre-booked birthday present from his parents.

He and his best friend Wills, alongside the day's other visitors, were being shown the most interesting parts of the tunnels by the tour guide, a tall elderly man with a beard.

He explained how they were built and ventilated; how to access them; and, even more fascinating, how a new town had evolved below the existing one.

The guide said: "I'm glad to see you've all got sturdy walking shoes on. It can be a bit rough underfoot in certain places."

He added: "I know it's summertime, but you will probably notice it's a bit colder in here than outside. In fact, the temperature is a constant 11C degrees throughout the tunnels. So, it may appear cold in summer but warm in winter."

Tom wanted to know how people managed to see in the darkness. "Was there any electricity down here?" he asked the guide.

"Interesting question. When the first section of tunnel, between West Harbour and Queen

Street, was opened it had batteries and a generator, but the rest of the network had to rely on the town supply, which was erratic at times.

"Eventually the council provided 200 hurricane lamps, which had glass shades protecting them from sudden draughts."

It was Wills who put the next question: "How did the people who stayed underground all the time know what was happening in the outside world?"

"Another good question, young man," said the guide. "There was actually a system of loudspeakers to relay wireless programmes as well as public announcements."

Tom was keen to find out more: "Could the Tunnel Town people do what they liked, or were there rules they had to follow?"

"Well, as each new section was opened it received an allocation of local people, with strict regulations enforced," replied the guide.

Keeping up with the news: an example of how life underground continued as near normal as possible, with the help of a newspaper seller. Note the abandoned Victorian railway line.

"Smoking was forbidden, and pets and prams were not allowed underground."

Wills turned to Tom: "I don't think my great-grandad would have liked it. Apparently, he loved smoking cigarettes, sometimes cigars, and he wouldn't have been happy with that rule."

Tom reflected: "Yes, it must have been unpopular as a lot more people used to smoke in those days. It's amazing to think that the link between cigarettes and lung cancer had not been established in the 1930s and 1940s.

"Surprisingly, some magazine adverts even featured doctors promoting the health benefits of certain cigarette brands. It's hard to believe - but true."

By now, the boys' attention had drifted away from the guided tour and focused instead on a large black bird that was circling above the group of visitors.

When the bird landed on a wooden table near where they stood, it didn't take them long to work out it was Ravi; a distinctive tag on his left leg clearly identified him as a one-time Tower of London raven.

He was pushing a metal tube around on the tabletop, rolling it back and forth with his beak. It was difficult to make out what was written on the tube as the lettering had faded, but it didn't look out of place in the shabby wartime surroundings.

Suddenly, a young child escaped his mum's grasp, slipped between his dad's legs and made a grab for the tube.

Ravi was having none of it. In a flash, he scooped up the tube in his beak and transported it high above the gaggle of people.

They all stood, necks bent, mouths agape, staring up at a ledge on the chalk wall where Ravi had landed. It was a place only accessible to winged visitors - or, possibly, a brave human with a long ladder.

Ravi fixed his dark, beady eyes on the gawping crowd. The raven was the clear winner in this staring match!

"Looks like Ravi's got a safe location for that thing, whatever it is." No sooner had Tom made his observation than Ravi took to the air, without the tube. He flew out of the tunnel entrance towards the crowded Main Sands.

Boy in a bunk: Young Ken Gower gets ready for bed while his mum chats to him about their experiences in Tunnel Town. Many homeless families spent years down there.

Chapter 5

Ravi's surprise visitor

After their tunnel visit, the two lads were invited to the Greens' house, where Tilda and Evie were playing in the paddling pool.

It was a warm mid-summer evening; the sun had only just started its slow descent behind Pegwell Bay.

"Have you visited Ramsgate Tunnels since you moved down from London," Tom asked the sisters.

"No," said Evie "but we've passed the big entrance sign near the beach lots of times and wondered what it was all about."

"You must go," chipped in Wills, who gave the girls a quick summary of everything they had seen that morning.

"It's a bit spooky at first but once you get used to the surroundings it's like time-travelling into the past. A sort of history museum on our doorstep," he added.

Suddenly, the conversation was interrupted by a commotion high above the children, at the top of the old conifer tree in the next-door garden.

It was Ravi with another bird, which seemed about the same size and had feathers that were also a shiny black colour. Was it a nesting partner, or perhaps just a pal of Ravi's?

The pair were making as much din - mostly high-pitched croaking - as a whole flock of ravens!

"What's going on," wondered Evie. "I've never heard so much noise coming from Ravi's tree, and there's only two of them up there."

In fact, it was what usually happens when a couple of old friends meet up after not seeing each other for a long time. They get very excited, and the volume goes up.

"... and do you remember the crows who came to your farewell party in Kensington Gardens?" said Rikki. "Well, they all send their best wishes. But the pigeons don't!" he added, with a chuckle.

"That's no surprise," said Ravi. "I never liked them. They always thought they were the best.

"It was typical of them to invite themselves to my leaving party. And, as usual, the tourists made more fuss about them than all the other birds who came, including those colourful parakeets."

"OK Ravi, calm down. That's all in the past now. You don't have to get worked up about the pigeons in Ramsgate. The seagulls are in charge down here," added Rikki.

"That's true. Anyway, enough of London, I want to show you around my new town. I have discovered some great spots for grabbing grub, including fish 'n' chips and pizzas dropped near the marina.

"And there's a very interesting cave behind the beach. I want you to tell me what you think of something I found there."

In a whirl of jet-black wings, the pair were off, quickly gaining height as they headed towards the marina and beyond.

They stopped to re-fuel on abandoned chips outside Peter's Fish Factory before continuing to the Main Sands and the entrance to Ramsgate Tunnels.

"It's a strange place," Ravi told his friend. "I found it one day when I saw a group of humans emerge from the bottom of the cliff face under a big red sign. I flew in to explore and was surprised to find other people in there.

"They were studying the old railway tunnel and stuff connected with trains.

"But there were also bunk beds, chairs and other bits of old furniture, which were all crammed into tiny rooms with walls created from flimsy wooden panels, covered with sheets and curtains. The rooms looked cosy, like human versions of our nests."

"I see what you mean," said Rikki after landing on the edge of a dusty tin, full of stubby bits of candle. "Where is that thing you wanted me to see?"

"Follow me, over here… "

Ravi flew off to a chalky shelf next to one of several side-tunnels branching off the main one. On top lay a metal tube with faded writing on it.

Rikki, bobbing his head up and down so he could get a better view, was intrigued. "What is it? Do you do anything with it," he asked his pal.

"Sometimes, I use it as a store for bits of food. I drop berries in and tip up the tube so that they roll down inside. Sometimes, when I've emptied it, I peck it and play a tune to myself.

"Occasionally, I leave the tube here overnight when the tunnels are closed. But this evening I think I'll take it back to my nest."

Later, after the birds had returned to the

garden next door to the Greens' home, Tilda and Evie realised that Ravi still had another raven with him. They were standing on Evie's bed looking out of a sloping skylight on the roof of their top-floor bedroom.

"Hey, sis, you can see from here that those two have got nests in separate trees. It doesn't look like they are a couple," said Evie.

"Or maybe they've had an argument," joked Tilda. "Like mum and dad do occasionally."

"I think they are probably just good mates who have had enough of each other's company after a long day together," said Evie.

"You mean a bit like us," quipped Tilda to her sister as they climbed into their beds, before turning off their lamps.

Chapter 6

Library link to lost cigar?

As he often did, Wills had dropped in to see his grandad on the way home from school that afternoon.

He got on so well with his Pops. They were both keen on sport, particularly football, and would happily discuss recent matches they had seen on TV. Currently, England's progress in the Euro tournament was the big talking point.

But today, Wills was more excited about the time he had spent in the Tunnels.

"Oh yes," explained Pops. "My dad was one of the original 'Tunnel Rats'. That's what they called the children who scurried around the network of passages. Not in a nasty way, though.

"Dad told me stories about how the kids

loved scampering about, playing hide 'n' seek and always getting up to some mischief. Tunnel Rats was just a friendly way of describing what the adults must have felt about them."

"Yes, I can understand that Pops. Did your dad ever mention them playing football in the tunnels?"

"No, he didn't. There really wasn't enough room for that, it was fairly cramped down there. I think they spent a lot of time playing cards and board games such as snakes 'n' ladders. Scrabble didn't come to England until after the war, in the 1950s."

"What else did he tell you, Pops? Did he find any interesting things in the tunnels?"

"A few things. I remember he kept an old pair of scissors that he had picked up near where a barber used to cut hair. They were very rusty, but he said they reminded him of the war years, so he never threw them away. Before he died, he passed them on to me."

"OK. Now for an easy question. Will England beat Ukraine in the Euro quarter-final on Saturday?"

"Definitely," enthused Pops. "And my forecast is that it will be a much easier match than against Germany."

"Fingers crossed," added his grandson as he made his way to the front door.

Suddenly, Pops shouted down the hallway as Wills was about to leave for home.

"Actually Wills, before you go, there was something else my dad treasured from his time in the tunnels. I nearly forgot. He once gave me a cigar, years after the war had ended. Not to smoke, of course, but as a memento, a keepsake."

"Why did he do that? Was there something special about it?" asked Wills.

"Well, he always believed that the cigar belonged to our famous wartime leader, Winston Churchill. Someone my dad knew must have picked it up where Churchill had dropped it when he was on a visit to Ramsgate after the town was heavily bombed in 1940.

"The man who found it passed it on to my dad as he knew how interested he was in wartime memorabilia."

"That's amazing. Where is the cigar now?" asked Wills.

"I don't know. I wish I did. I suspect it would probably be worth a lot of money today, even though a bit of it had been smoked.

"I gave it to the town library when they were holding an exhibition in 1994 on the 50th anniversary of the D-Day landings. I'm not sure what they did with it.

"I just presumed they had stored it away in their archives somewhere. Maybe it went up in flames when that terrible fire destroyed most of the library ten years later."

As Wills' grandad reflected on the past, it jogged his memory about related tales.

"I remember reading a newspaper story a couple of years ago about the time Churchill had dropped a part-smoked cigar outside the London Coliseum in Westminster where he and his wife were attending a film premiere in 1953.

"It was picked up by a cinema usherette who was so excited by her find that she wrote to 10 Downing Street to ask the PM's permission to tell her friends about it. She got a polite reply from Churchill telling her it was alright.

"Anyway, a relative of the woman recently put the cigar up for auction, along with Churchill's response letter to the usherette, plus a cutting from the Daily Telegraph in 1953 about the original find. Together, the lot fetched £4,800."

Pops was now warming to the subject. He told Wills a similar story about a cigar butt discarded by Churchill in the 1940s. A policeman had picked it up and he had passed it on to his grandson. When he eventually put it up for auction last year, it fetched £4,270."

The following morning, as the Green sisters made their way to school with the boys, Wills was buzzing with excitement as he told them about his grandad's cigar stories.

"Wow! All that money just for the remains of a cigar. They weren't even new ones. Why do adults pay so much for rubbish?" demanded Tom.

Tilda was quick to fire back: "It depends on who owned the 'rubbish' in the first place, Tom. The fact it belonged to Winston Churchill means it is very rare and worth much more than if it belonged to the local butcher, for instance."

"Ok, I understand" said Tom "but the problem is that none of us has a clue what happened to Churchill's Ramsgate cigar."

He turned to Wills: "All we know is what your grandad told you, that it ended up at the library."

Tom said: "Maybe that should be our starting point. Let's go at the weekend and find out if anyone remembers the exhibition."

Chapter 7

A wild goose chase?

The following morning at school, it was the second history lesson of the week for Wills, Tom and Evie. Mr Smith was giving the class advance notice of a project for them to do during the summer holidays.

"What I want from you is the best wartime story connected with where you live. That might be about what happened to local children who were evacuated to safer places. Where did they go? How did that affect their education?

"Or it could be something connected to the rescue of troops from Dunkirk in northern France and the role that Ramsgate's Little Ships played in that famous event."

Mr Smith added: "It's probably worth you

talking to relatives who remember the war years or, more likely, those relatives who were once told by older adults about their experiences."

"It would be even better if you can illustrate your project, with artwork or photographs."

Wills' desk was next to Evie's near the back of the classroom. He had already told her about the chat with his grandad the previous day.

He turned to her: "Do you think Mr Smith would be happy with a project on Pops' pair of rusty scissors from the tunnels?"

"I don't think that would cut it!" she winked.

That Saturday morning, the four friends turned up at the library shortly after it opened. They were keen to get on with their enquiries.

"We're looking for a cigar," blurted Wills in the direction of the receptionist, who was studying something on her computer screen.

"I'm sorry," she said, looking up from her desk. "Did you say a cigar? You do know this is a library, don't you?"

Tom stepped up to the counter. "Actually, it's one that Winston Churchill threw away when he was here during the war. We think it was part of a library exhibition and you might still have it?"

"I'm not sure I know what you're referring to," replied the receptionist. "I only started here a few weeks ago. I'll fetch my colleague; she might be able to help."

The children stared at each other as they waited, wondering if they would get the answer they wanted.

After several minutes, another woman appeared. "Hello, I'm the head librarian. My colleague explained the purpose of your visit. Something to do with a cigar.

"Yes, we did have an exhibition to mark the 50th anniversary of D-Day landings but it was before I started here and I'm not sure anyone who works here now will have any knowledge of what happened to all the exhibits. I'm sorry to disappoint you."

That afternoon, Tilda and Evie wore sad expressions on their faces as they explained to their parents the unsuccessful outcome of their morning trip.

"It sounds like a wild goose chase to me," said their dad.

"What are you talking about? We're not looking for a goose" said Tilda, indignantly.

"Well, that's what is called an idiom, or a saying. It means a frustrating search that usually involves a big waste of time."

"Aw dad, I thought you would be a bit more positive than that. It's really important that we find the cigar. It might be worth a lot of money and, besides, it would make a great story for our history project."

"I understand, Tilda, and maybe I can help. I could post a story on our newspaper website asking for any information readers may have about the cigar mystery." Mike Green had been a journalist on the Thanet Gazette since the family moved to Ramsgate four years ago.

He added: "I'll explain about the cigar's last known location at the library, but I won't mention your theory about its possible worth.

"It can't do any harm. You never know, we might strike lucky. In which case, our website would be the goose that laid the golden egg - that's another goose idiom, Tilda!"

"Haha. Very funny, dad."

Meanwhile, a few houses down the road from the Greens, Ravi had dropped in to see Tom. He wanted him to meet Rikki, his friend from London.

"You saved my life," croaked Ravi. "Thank you. Saved my life."

"Wow, did you hear that!" Tom was shouting to his mum who was watering flowers in the garden. "Ravi has just repeated what I keep saying to him on his morning visits. That's amazing."

"My life. Thank you. Thank you." There

seemed to be no stopping Ravi. He was in full flow.

"He is a talkative bird today," said Tom's mum. "I think he deserves a special treat." She disappeared into the kitchen.

Tom noticed something he had not seen earlier. On the far side of the lawn, where Ravi and Rikki had first landed, there was a tube. He was sure he had seen it somewhere before but couldn't remember where.

His mum reappeared from the back door with two small pieces of chicken in her gloved hand. She placed the meat on the concrete flags. It was a meal Ravi and Rikki could not resist. They tore at the flesh with great gusto.

After a while, Ravi's head bobbed up. "Thank you. Saved my life."

He waddled across the lawn, wrapped his beak around the tube and flew off towards the sea front. Rikki finished the last of his chicken and set off in the same direction.

"That is one clever bird," said Tom to his mum. "I'll have to teach him to say some other things as well."

Chapter 8

'I love my Romeo & Juliet'

"The wonders of social media," proclaimed Mike to a couple of colleagues at his newspaper office.

"Remember me telling you about the Churchill cigar mystery. I posted an appeal for information on our Facebook page and I have just received a very interesting reply."

"Don't tell me, Mike," smirked the younger of the two reporters, "someone found it in their attic but they're not sure if it's genuine as it was in a box with a sticker on it saying: 'Grandad's magic tricks'."

"No, clever clogs, this is serious," Mike fired back. "The guy is a member of the Marzetti family. He is a distant relative of the man who ran the Marzetti Popular Hotel in Harbour Parade during the 1930s and '40s.

"You two probably don't know your Ramsgate history, but that was the hotel that Churchill visited after it had been badly damaged during a bombing raid.

"There's a good photograph of him emerging from the hotel. You could see the smashed front windows."

"OK, Mike, but what's that got to do with the cigar?" wondered the second reporter.

"Not so much the cigar, but the tube it was in," Mike replied.

He went on to explain that he had messaged the helpful Marzetti relative, asking him to get back in touch. They then had a long phone conversation about what his family knew about the wartime incident.

Mr Marzetti had apparently followed Churchill out of his hotel premises and saw him throw the tube in a litter bin after lighting his cigar. The hotelier waited until Churchill and his officials were out of sight, then fished the tube out of the bin.

Not surprisingly, it was only Mr Marzetti who showed any interest in Churchill's cast-off. Apparently, he kept the tube on display in the hotel reception area after it had been renovated. But nobody was impressed as it was a reminder of the terrible event that had led to the prime minister making his visit.

Mr Marzetti realised it was probably not good for business, so he moved the tube to the bathroom and kept his toothbrush propped up in it, near the wash basin. But his wife objected and said it was unhygienic.

Finally, he decided to keep it in his sock drawer where no one could see it apart from him. Every time he put on a new pair he would kiss the tube for good luck.

Mike continued: "One detail that caught my attention was that the relative remembered something Mr Marzetti said whenever he had the cigar tube in his hand: 'I love my Romeo and Juliet'.

"He wasn't sure why the old man said that. Maybe it was the name of a cigar brand, possibly from Italy. Marzetti's name certainly sounds like he was of Italian origin, and Shakespeare's most famous play was set in the Italian city of Verona.

"There must have been some sort of link between the tube and Romeo and Juliet."

The older reporter had been listening closely to the story. "That's all very interesting, Mike, but it's not going to help us fill this week's newspaper!

"Perhaps we should ring the fire service to see if they have rescued any cats from trees!" he jested. "There's more chance of that making it into the Gazette than Mr Marzetti's missing tube."

Mike did not like the suggestion that he was wasting his time, but eventually admitted:

"You're probably right. The last thing the relative told me was that all Mr Marzetti's possessions, including his sock drawer, had been cleared when he went into a care home, aged 90. The chances are the tube has been lost without trace."

That evening, after their family meal, Mike updated his daughters on the latest information.

Evie thought it was a positive development. "At least we know the cigar tube wasn't thrown out with the rubbish in 1940 and that it survived the war with the help of Mr Marzetti. Who knows, it may yet turn up in an unexpected place."

Tilda added: "Dad, you got a result when you reached out on Facebook. It might not have been everything we wanted but at least it has started a conversation about the subject.

"Perhaps you could post a piece about the Romeo and Juliet thing - and see if you get any response. As you said before, it's worth a try."

"I'll do that, girls. But I'm still puzzled because Italy is not famous for producing cigars. Spaghetti bolognese and lasagne, yes, but cigars, no."

Chapter 9

Cuba is the clue

Who would have thought it? England were to face Italy after heroically progressing to the final of Euro 2020.

Following a comfortable win against Ukraine in the quarter-finals, the Three Lions went on to beat Denmark in the semi-finals after extra time.

England's big moment had arrived. It was 55 years since they had lifted the World Cup, and this was the chance for glory in a major competition after so many disappointments.

Wills was at his grandad's to watch the match live. Pops had also invited Tom as well as Tilda and Evie. The sisters were not big football fans, but this was different. The whole country would be tuned in. It was history in the making.

They all sat in front of Pops' TV waiting excitedly for the kick-off at 8pm.

Down the road, near the top of an old conifer tree, the atmosphere could not have been more different.

Ravi and Rikki had experienced the wild behaviour of humans over recent weeks and were wary that something similar could happen that night. They recognised the early signs of a repeat performance: cars honking their horns, flags being waved for no apparent reason, and very loud talking outside buildings where, it seemed, everyone was drinking.

"It looks like there's another one tonight," said Ravi. "This has gone on for so long. When will it stop? It used to be so peaceful here.

"Ramsgate was such a pleasant change after all the noise of London. But then, all the humans started to go crazy every few days, letting off fireworks, shouting and screaming.

"Worst of all, they are keeping us awake when

it's time to sleep."

"Chill, my friend," said Rikki. "It's probably some strange festival that happens every few years. It will come to an end soon, I'm sure. The humans will be walking around in a daze tomorrow, all looking as miserable as usual."

Lo and behold! That is exactly what came to pass. The four children walked to school the Monday after the match, with not a lot to say. There was no more honking of car horns and the adults had sour expressions on their faces.

"Ah, peace at last," observed Rikki as he watched the youngsters from his tree branch.

"I just wish the seagulls could be as silent as the humans," replied Ravi.

"Trust you to bring that up again," quipped Rikki.

Not far away, Mike was at his desk checking emails and social media feeds.

"Wow, I've struck gold," he exclaimed to himself. Alone in his office, he was reading a message from an official at the International Churchill Society (ICS) who had replied to his weekend post.

The message said: "Mike, I can understand your confusion. Italy is not the clue; Cuba is the clue."

Mike, still confused, read on. "It's not Romeo and Juliet; it's Romeo y Julieta - the Spanish version of their names. And that is the brand name of a famous cigar in Cuba, where Spanish is the main language.

"The final piece in the jigsaw is that these were Churchill's favourite cigars. So, it is very likely that the tube you refer to had contained a cigar belonging to him.

"Put it like this, I can't imagine anyone in wartime Ramsgate being able to afford or having access to the sort of top-quality Cuban cigars that Churchill favoured."

Mike leant back in his chair, hands behind his head. He imagined how delighted his girls would be when he went home to tell them the news.

But first, he needed to reply to the man at the Churchill Society thanking him for this vital piece of information.

Then, Mike thought: "All that remains to do now is to find the tube. A bit like looking for a needle in a haystack!"

Chapter 10

The search hots up

"So, that is a bit of a breakthrough," said Tamara after her husband had explained about Romeo y Julieta to the family as they sat round the dining table.

Tilda looked at Evie. They both had the same thought. The girls spluttered out words in their rush to reveal what they had not bothered to tell their parents two weeks ago. At the time it had not seemed relevant.

Evie spoke first: "One morning, Ravi turned up at school with a tube in his beak and he interrupted Mr Smith's history lesson by tapping it on the classroom window. It caused a big distraction and Mr Smith wasn't happy at all.

"Anyway, when we saw the boys shortly

afterwards, they told us they had seen Ravi with the tube during their visit to Ramsgate Tunnels and that it had something written on it that they couldn't read as the lettering was faded."

Tilda followed up: "That could be the Romeo and Juliet tube, or whatever it is in Spanish. Tom said it looked really old and a bit battered. I think we should talk to him and Wills about how we can track down the tube."

"OK girls," said their mum. "But be very careful. We don't want anyone falling from a tree or doing anything you shouldn't be doing in the tunnels."

Evie sad: "Don't be silly mum, we're only going in search of Ravi to see if he can lead us to the tube."

"Yes, but we know what happened when Tom last went looking for Ravi, on the coast path. He fell down the cliff and nearly died."

"Alright mum," said Tilda. "We promise we won't take any risks and we'll make sure the boys don't either."

"I'll keep my fingers crossed - and my toes," added mum with a grin.

The next day, Mike received a call in his office from the manager at the town's library. She explained she had spoken to four children when they visited recently, in connection with a cigar.

"Yes, that's right," said Mike. "I'm Mr Green, the dad of the two girls. They're my daughters, Tilda and Evie. Has something happened?"

"Well, one of our former staff members dropped in at the library yesterday. George - that's his name - had read something about you wanting information about a cigar of Churchill's that was in an exhibition here nearly 30 years ago.

"Apparently, he was still working at the library when there was a catastrophic blaze in 2004. The fire service did the best they could, but we lost the entire book stock, either burnt or badly damaged by smoke or water.

"However, there was a windowless storeroom

on the ground floor that suffered less damage and its contents remained mostly intact."

Mike interjected: "Go on, I'm intrigued. What did they find in there?"

"George returned to the building - or what was left of it - a couple of days after it was declared safe. He was rummaging around in the storeroom and found a large metal box. It had cooled sufficiently for him to open it. Inside, he discovered a small exhibition case containing the remains of a cigar. It still had a paper band around the unsmoked end. I think George said the band had the maker's name on it."

On the other end of the phone, Mike was almost speechless with excitement. But he stayed calm enough to make no mistake in writing down the contact details for George.

"Thank you so much. Wait until I tell my daughters. This will definitely make their day."

Chapter 11

A plan takes shape

Wills was sitting in his garden on a wooden bench overlooking the lawn. His bad mood was shared by Tom as they chatted about the result of the England match at the weekend.

"I just can't believe we lost after scoring so early. We were well on top of the Italy team but we should have made sure of the win by getting a second goal. And when it went to penalties at the end of extra time, we all knew what was going to happen."

Tom agreed, adding: "I felt really sorry for that young player who missed the last penalty. He had been brought on as a substitute only a few minutes earlier and had not had enough time to get into his stride.

"He had spent so long on the subs bench he was probably nervous when he finally came onto the pitch."

Their reflections on the Wembley game were suddenly interrupted by the arrival of Evie and Tilda.

"Come on, boys, it's only a football match," said Evie who had guessed the subject of their conversation from the grim look on their faces.

"Anyway," chipped in Tilda, "let's look on the bright side. Dad was telling us some important information about the tube and how there's a good chance it is was the one thrown away by Winston Churchill."

Evie said: "It's a shame we didn't realise the connection when Ravi dropped the tube under our classroom window after Mr Smith scared him away. Now we don't know where to start looking. It could be anywhere."

Wills was quick to reply: "I think I know where it could be. The other day, Ravi landed on the lawn with a tube in his beak." He pointed to the spot, on the far side of the grass.

"He was here with that pal of his. After mum fed them some bits of chicken, Ravi hopped over the lawn and picked up the tube and flew off towards the seafront."

"That makes sense, Wills," said Tom. "Remember when we saw him in the tunnels and he was messing about with a similar looking tube. Eventually he took off with it and landed on a high shelf on the wall."

Tom continued: "So, if there is just one tube - and not more than one - we just need to track down Ravi and wait for an opportunity to get our hands on it.

"That might not be easy," observed Tilda. "Especially if he keeps it at the top of his tree or leaves it on a ledge in the tunnels, both of which are out of reach."

But Wills said: "He might return to our garden with it. If so, I'm sure we could distract him with a tasty morsel and make our move while he's eating it."

The four of them formed a plan which involved each keeping an eye out for the raven and making a note of the times and places he had the tube with him.

Also, they should all have a couple of treats in their pockets so that, if an opportunity arose, like the one in Wills' garden, they could tempt Ravi to leave the tube unguarded.

It was teatime for the children, so they made their separate ways home with high hopes of their quest ending successfully.

* * * *

For two days, the children kept a close watch on Ravi's movements. He was spotted in the Greens' garden and in their neighbours' tree; he continued to follow them to school and he had spent time with Wills in his garden, but on none of these occasions did Ravi have the tube with him.

"Ravi is not being very cooperative," said Tom as he and Wills tried to figure out what to do next.

Wills produced a Smarties tube from his jacket pocket. "I've got an idea. I'm not sure it will work but it's worth a try."

He emptied the sweets into his hand and poured them into his pocket. Then he placed the tube on the garden table. The boys went inside the house and upstairs to Wills' bedroom to observe the scene below.

After half an hour of waiting without any sign of Ravi, Wills turned to Tom. "I'm going down to the kitchen to get something from the fridge. You stay here and give me a shout if he appears in the garden."

Downstairs, Wills reached into the store cupboard to grab a packet of oatmeal biscuits before pulling on the fridge door and delving into the chiller section. "That's what I need," he said to himself as he picked up a large plastic box containing the joint of beef set aside for the weekend roast meal.

"What are you doing?" His mum's unexpected voice made him jump.

"Oh, hi mum. Tom and I are trying to train Ravi to fetch the tube from where he keeps it. The one we think belonged to Winston Churchill. Remember, we told you about it the other day."

"Yes, I do remember. But where are you taking our Sunday dinner? What's that got to do with Ravi?" asked his mum, in a stern voice.

"Ah well, I read somewhere that a favourite treat for ravens is a biscuit soaked in blood. In fact, that's what the raven master at the Tower of London gives his birds sometimes."

"I know what you have in mind," replied his mum. "But I don't think you need the whole chunk of meat! I'll drain some of the blood from the container and put it in a little pot. Then you can dip the biscuit into the blood."

"Great, thanks mum. I'll take it to my bedroom. Hopefully, Ravi will make an appearance soon."

Chapter 12

Hopes of a happy ending

By now, Mike had contacted George, the retired library assistant, and made plans to meet him at his home on Ramsgate's Nethercourt estate the following morning.

Mike had updated Tamara, but the couple had decided not to tell their daughters until there was positive evidence of the Churchill cigar.

"Besides," said Tamara, "they are excited enough about that tube without further complicating things."

After breakfast the next day, Mike set off for work. In the office, he explained to his editor who he was going to see, and why.

"Take your camera with you, Mike. This could be a big story if all the parts fall into place, and we will need photos of all the people involved," his boss said.

Ten minutes later, Mike parked his car outside George's house. He was greeted on the path by an elderly man with a welcoming smile. "Step inside, Mr Green. Tea or coffee?"

"Tea, milk, no sugar, thank you. And please call me Mike."

As the journalist made himself comfortable, he noticed a small wooden box on the arm of the settee.

"Is that it?" asked Mike, pointing to the box, as George returned with a mug of tea and a plate of biscuits.

"Yes, it used to contain an old set of dominoes, but I gave them to my grandchildren to play with. I kept the box as I thought it would be ideal for the cigar," explained George, passing it to Mike for him to inspect.

He slid its lid off to reveal a fluffy bed of cotton wool on which the cigar rested.

"It's seen better days," laughed Mike as he stared at the crushed end of the once-perfect Cuban cigar.

"Yes, of course," replied George. "But if what we have been told is true, it was the heel of Churchill's shoe which left it in that state, when he was told to put it out before going into the tunnels."

"It's a remarkable story, George. We also believe that the tube it was in might still be in Ramsgate. If that also turns up, I will make every effort to verify the authenticity of both the cigar and its tube. Then, we could decide what to do with them next."

George said: "I'm happy for you to do that. But on one condition - that the cigar remains in Ramsgate."

"That would be my wish, too," replied Mike. But let's take it one step at a time. The first step will be to seek expert opinion, to authenticate what we've got."

The two men agreed that Mike would make enquiries and keep George informed about progress.

Before leaving, Mike took another look inside the old dominoes box. "I see the band is still on the cigar," he said.

"It's a Romeo y Julieta and that was Winston's favourite, so I understand," replied George.

"Yes, but let's hope this story ends more happily than it did for Romeo and Juliet in Shakespeare's play," added Mike.

On that note, the two shook hands and Mike walked down the path to his waiting car.

Chapter 13

Nice one Winston

The long wait for Ravi continued at Wills' house. The raven had not been seen for days near the Greens' home either, nor had his pal Rikki, and Ravi was not even following the children to school in the mornings.

What they didn't know was that the two birds had gone on a short break away from Ramsgate. The noisy seagulls were irritating Ravi, so Rikki had suggested they fly inland to get away from the birds' squawking.

Understandably, Tilda and Evie were getting worried that the ravens had left the area and might never return. That could mean them not being able to track down the little metal tube, on which they were pinning their hopes.

Their parents were aware of the girls' disappointment and decided to tell them the news about George and his box, if Ravi did not appear by the weekend.

In the meantime, the sisters did have something else to distract them. Tomorrow was Friday, which meant 'basket night' in the Green household.

This had become a family tradition that involved a small wicker basket, filled with sweets, being left at the bottom of the stairs at about 7pm by their mum or dad.

When one of them rang a little blue bell, it was the signal for Tilda or Evie - whoever's turn it was - to run down from their bedroom and collect the basket, before returning upstairs to share the goodies.

However, there was one condition: the girls must not be seen or heard again until the following morning. That way, Mike and Tamara had a peaceful evening, uninterrupted.

"At least we can look forward to that," said Tilda to her sister as they curled up in their beds on Thursday night.

"Yes, but I do hope Ravi is still in this area. We would miss him so much, he's such a character."

Ten houses down the road from where the girls lived, Wills was sat at his bedroom desk putting the final touches to his plan to 'persuade' Ravi - if he ever returned - to bring the cigar tube back to his garden.

He was applying a coat of light grey paint to the cardboard Smarties tube to cover up all its bright colours and make it look more like the metal version.

After he had finished, he placed the tube in an empty ice cream carton alongside a couple of oatmeal biscuits and the small pot of blood.

He jumped into bed and crossed his fingers, before turning off his lamp.

When Wills awoke, it was a glorious sunny

morning. His first thought, however, was that it was now four days since Ravi had made a visit to his lawn.

"Good morning, mum." Wills was walking to the back door when she came into the kitchen. "I'm going to lay the tube on the grass today. I've painted it so Ravi will think it's the real thing."

"What happens then?" his mum asked.

"As you know, Ravi and I are good friends, so when he picks up the tube he won't mind me approaching him.

"I'll drop a piece of the blood-soaked biscuit near him and I'm sure he will drop the tube.

"Then - and this is the important bit - when he's gobbling the bickie, I'll say to him: 'Nice one Winston' several times to make a link in his brainy brain between him dropping the tube and getting the reward of a tasty biscuit. Then, I'll pick up the tube and pocket it."

His mum suddenly turned towards the kitchen window. "Look, my dear, that is very good timing. A bird with shiny black feathers has just landed on the lawn. Time to put your plan into practice!"

Wills crept out of the door and across the path to the edge of the grass.

"Saved your life. Saved your life," croaked Ravi.

"He is in a talkative mood today," thought Wills, "He might like the idea of learning a new phrase."

As planned, Wills placed the blood-soaked biscuit in front of Ravi who immediately dropped the tube in exchange for the biscuit.

"Nice one Winston. Nice one Winston. Nice one Winston," chirped Wills.

"Saved your Winston. Saved your Winston" came the reply from Ravi.

At this point, Wills' mum, who had overheard the chatter, emerged from the house. "He got things a bit mixed up, but it was still an excellent first lesson."

Chapter 14

Basket night treat

Rikki realised straight away there was a problem, and he knew Ravi would not be happy.

Earlier that afternoon, when he and Ravi were flying home from their short break they had decided to split up when they arrived in Ramsgate. Ravi would return to Wills' house while Rikki would fly to the seafront and collect the tube from the tunnels.

Ravi had left the tube there, knowing that it was full of berries and insects which they could have as a meal that evening.

So, when he saw Rikki descend from the sky and land in Wills' garden, without the tube, it was clear something had gone wrong.

"What's the problem, my friend?"

Rikki explained: "I arrived at the tunnels and found the tube but when I picked it up it slipped out of my beak and rolled into a gap between the ledge and the wall. The more I tried to free it with my claw the more it got stuck in the gap.

"It will need two of us to try to release it. If not, we'll just have to leave it there. I'm sure no one will miss it - and we're sure to find another one somewhere."

In fact, Rikki did not have to wait long. "Look, Ravi, there's one over there on the grass!"

"No Rikki, leave it where it is, please. Before you got here, I was given a blood-soaked biscuit after I dropped that tube. I've not had one of those since I was thrown out of the Tower. Mmm, it was delicious."

Ravi continued: "Maybe it's a special tube. Or maybe all tubes are special to the humans. When I was eating the biscuit, the boy said something about "Winston" and he seemed very pleased when I tried to repeat it."

Wills and his mum, who were now back in the house, heard the ravens jabbering away outside but of course they had no idea what it was all about. They didn't understand bird-speak.

Soon, the two birds took off and flew south towards the beach, then headed in the direction of the tunnels' entrance under the Eastcliff.

Once inside, the ravens, sitting on a ledge high above a group of visitors, stared at the tube wedged firmly in a small crack, probably created by workmen hacking away at the chalky rock over a hundred years ago.

Ravi took charge of the situation. "Before we can pull it free we will have to peck at the chalk near the end of the tube which is most stuck. That should help to release it and then we can have a go at forcing it out with our claws."

"Sounds like a good plan," agreed Rikki.

Fortunately, the chalk was soft enough for the ravens to chip away little fragments. Bit by bit they made enough space around the tube to get their claws under it and to lever it clear of the wall.

"Success," exclaimed Ravi triumphantly. "Let's take it back to my tree and have our meal. It's been a hard day and we need some rest."

That evening, Tilda and Evie spotted the two feathered friends high up in the conifer tree from their bedroom window overlooking the neighbours' garden.

Evie said: "They seem happy enough. Looks like they've got something to eat. But I can't see the tube."

Tilda smiled: "At least we know they've not left the area, which was our main concern. Let's catch up with Wills and see if he has anything to report."

After the sisters had told their parents they were going down the road to see Wills for a chat, Mike, who had just returned from work, took the opportunity to update his wife.

"It's great news, Tamara. I caught a train to

London this morning so I could meet the guy from the International Churchill Society who I was in touch with recently. Because he knew I was bringing George's cigar he had arranged for an expert from the Guild of Cigar Manufacturers to join us.

"He spent a long time using his instruments to work out the approximate age of the cigar. Apparently, it's a bit like telling how old a tree is. All very clever science, way over my head!

"Anyway, the upshot is that the cigar is of Cuban origin, with a genuine Romeo y Julieta paper band wrapped around it and, according to the expert, it is highly likely to be from a batch made exclusively for Winston Churchill at the start of the war."

"That is truly amazing," said Tamara. "As a celebration, I think the girls should get extra sweets in their basket tonight."

Chapter 15

The biscuit trick

When Tilda and Evie arrived at Wills' house there was no sign of either Ravi or Rikki.

As the three youngsters gathered around the garden table in the early evening sun, Wills explained how his trial run of the plan to get his hands on the tube - with the help of Ravi - had worked out well.

"The blood-soaked biscuit is a winner," he exclaimed. "Ravi was like a child in a sweetshop, he couldn't get enough of it. No wonder he dropped the tube as soon as he saw the biscuit."

But Tilda saw a problem. "What if Ravi thinks he only needs to pick up the painted Smarties tube to get his reward? He might never fly here with the cigar tube."

"Yes, I had thought of that. What I'm going to do is continue to teach him to associate getting a reward with that tube." Wills pointed across the lawn to where Ravi had abandoned the Smarties tube. "Then I will hide it in the kitchen and leave it there.

"Hopefully, he will be so desperate to get his biscuit treat that he will bring the cigar tube here instead."

Evie was impressed. She patted Wills on the back: "Good thinking, professor!"

With that, the sisters went home. It was nearly six o'clock and time for tea, followed by basket night. "No time to waste," they agreed with a smile.

The following morning, the sisters scrambled downstairs and found their parents eating breakfast in the kitchen. Evie was holding the empty wicker basket. "They were scrummy, thank you both."

"Well, there was plenty to celebrate," replied

their dad. "And last night, I had an email from the International Churchill Society with a certificate of authentication attached.

"Basically, it confirms that the cigar I showed them in London this week has been officially verified as Churchill's."

"That's awesome, dad. Can we tell the boys?" asked Tilda.

"Yes, but please ask them to keep it between yourselves for the time being. We don't want everyone to know our secret. I'd rather let the world know in next week's Gazette.

"In the meantime, I'm going to see George to let him know the good news. He'll be delighted."

The girls finished their toast and jam, jumped down from their chairs and headed for the door.

They found Tom in Wills' garden, in the company of a very chirpy Ravi: "Nice one Winston. You saved my life. Thank you Winston", followed by numerous variations of the expressions Wills had repeated to him recently.

He explained: "Ravi came back early this morning and was wandering around the lawn with the Smarties tube in his beak. I could see him from my bedroom window. He looked a bit unhappy, so I dashed downstairs and prepared a biscuit for him.

"That did the trick! As soon as I appeared, he dropped the tube and snapped up the biscuit. He finished it and flew off. Now, I will remove the tube and keep it indoors," added Wills.

"You sound like a magician," said Tom. "As if you're about to pull a rabbit out of a hat!"

"Haha. No rabbit, just a cigar tube, hopefully" added Wills, crossing his fingers.

Their laughter was suddenly interrupted by the swoosh of wings. Ravi and Rikki descended onto the grass. It was Rikki carrying the tube - the one the children wanted: the cigar tube!

While they had been talking, Ravi had gone to fetch his pal to show him the biscuit trick. Rikki had been given the job of bringing the tube.

Wills ran inside to get another blood-soaked biscuit. When he re-appeared, Rikki placed the tube on the lawn and stared intently at the youngster with his pearl-black eyes.

Wills released the biscuit from his right hand and, in a flash, had the tube in his left hand.

"Job done," grinned Tom as the two ravens tucked into the last few crumbs.

But it was Ravi who had the last say: "Nice one Winston".

Chapter 16

The generous benefactor

A month later, Ravi was sitting proudly on his new perch - a metal tube suspended on two wires hanging from the ceiling of the main tunnel entrance. It wasn't the original cigar tube but a replica with Romeo y Julieta branding on it.

"It will make him feel at home," said Mike as he pointed his camera in the raven's direction to take a picture for the front page of that week's edition of the Gazette. "He fully deserves his place in such a historic story," he told George, his special guest for the afternoon.

The two men had just walked down to the tunnels from Ramsgate library. It was there that the national press, TV crews and radio teams had gathered for the unveiling of a steel and glass cabinet displaying the Churchill cigar, its tube, and the authentication certificate.

The three items had been sold as one lot at an auction held in the nearby city of Canterbury. Over £10,000 was paid by an anonymous bidder who later informed the library he wanted to honour George's wish that the Churchill collection should stay in Ramsgate.

He also said he would pay the costs of mounting a permanent exhibition in the building.

The official opening ceremony was attended by the Green family, plus Wills and Tom, as well as the town's mayor, council officials and dozens of invited guests.

"Who is Benny Factor?" Tilda asked her mum as she pointed at the front of the event programme.

"I thought you'd be puzzled by that. The man who has generously donated everything did not want to be identified. He is what you call a benefactor. In the programme he is listed as 'Benny Factor'. So he remains anonymous."

"He seems to have a good sense of humour." observed Evie. "And what a kind person he is."

"Yes, girls, what the world needs now is more people like Benny."

Acknowledgements

Thanks to Ramsgate Tunnels for allowing me to reproduce original photographs from the 1940s, and to Ramsgate Library for their assistance in my research of the Churchill cigar story.

9 781803 693682